A Special Day
The Day Eid Met Christmas

 W9-DFQ-068

Written by: Mahmoud ElZein
Illustrated by: Rania Hasan

Do you believe in magic,
that of kindness and love?

One year, Christmas and
Eid fell on the same day.

Do you believe in magic
That of Kindness and Love

Written by: Mahmoud ElZein.

Illustrated by: Rania Hasan.

Editorial Service: Lou Treleaven.

I dedicate this story to the children who inspire our hearts to leap into
a world of kindness and innocence.

Due thanks to my family for their lovely support.

M. Elzein

Copyright notice: Mahmoud ElZein, © August 12, 2020 -

All rights reserved. No part of this publication may be reproduced,
translated, distributed, or transmitted in any form or by any means,
including photocopying, recording, or other electronic or mechanical
methods, without the prior written permission of the author, Mahmoud
Elzein, except in the case of brief quotations embodied in book reviews.

For permission requests, write to the author at:
elzeinmahmoud@hotmail.com

All proceeds from the story and Book/ebook, and in other media forms,
in any language, belong solely to the author and are part of the author's
intellectual property.

On that special day, something magical happened...

To prepare for Christmas, Eva's school performed
a Christmas Carol for kids from the orphanage.
Later that night, Eva thought of the kids' cheers,
and she felt pure joy.

To celebrate Eid, Aya's school invited orphans for cake and lemonade.
Later that night, Aya fell asleep with a warm smile on her face.

The next morning, Eva and Aya went to the largest toy store in town.

The two girls bought their gifts and walked
into the elevator at the same time.
They looked with curiosity at each other's gift.
"Hi, I am Eva."
"Hi, I am Aya."

Suddenly, the lights went out, and the
elevator stopped.
Eva and Aya felt scared and quickly
hid behind their mothers.
Still, magically, destiny planted seeds of
friendship and love between the two
girls.

Eva tried to get their minds off the dark elevator, "Hey Aya! I like guessing games. Can you guess what's my gift?" Eva asked.

"I will give you a hint: It can't swim nor roll, but it can fly."

"A penguin?" Aya asked.
"Nooo! Penguins can't fly!"
Eva answered.

"A chicken?" Aya asked.
"Buck-buck-buck! Nooo!"
Eva said.

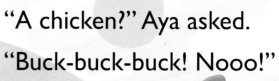

"Listen, it makes a buzzzzz sound,"
Eva hinted.

"Hmm, a buzzing bee!" Aya shouted.

"Wow! Good guess! It's a flying bee,"
Eva cheered.

"Now, it's my turn to guess!" Eva said.

"Here's my hint," Aya said, "It takes princesses places, but it's not a car, nor a boat."

"A horse?" Eva asked.

"Yee-haw. Nooo!" Aya answered.

"Hmm… I got it!" Eva excitedly said.
"It's a golden carriage, just like the one that Cinderella rides!"
"Bravooo! Princess Eva, bravo!"

After a few minutes, the lights came back on,
and the elevator slowly went down to the lobby.
When the girls left the store, they saw a road
banner that got them thinking of other kids.

"I feel really sad now," Eva whispered.

"Me too!" Aya said. "The orphans might not get any gifts!"

When the girls looked at each other, a single idea flashed through their minds. "Let's give our gifts away!" they said. The kindness of their hearts brightly lit up their faces.

"How about we exchange places when we give our gifts?" Eva asked.

"I love your idea!" Aya said. "Kids are kids, and it doesn't matter what their color, religion, or race is!"

"Girls! We are so happy and proud of you," their mothers said.

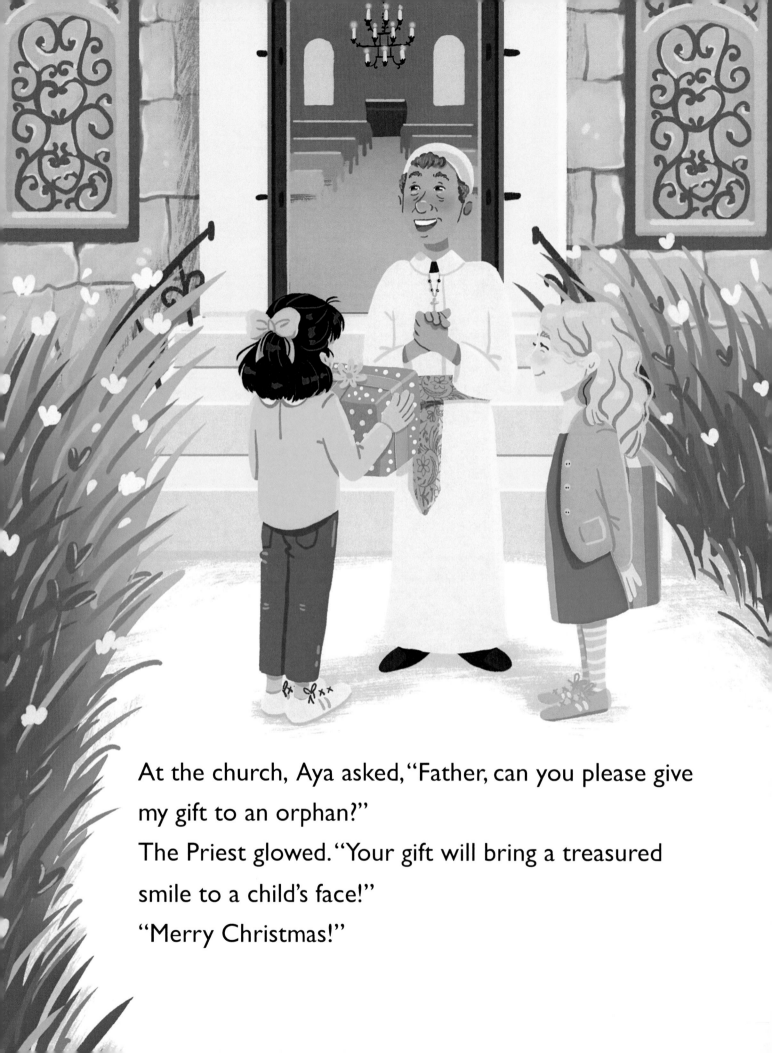

At the church, Aya asked, "Father, can you please give my gift to an orphan?"

The Priest glowed. "Your gift will bring a treasured smile to a child's face!"

"Merry Christmas!"

At the mosque, Eva asked, "Shaykh, can you please share my gift with an orphan?"

The Shaykh's face lit up. "Your act of kindness will inspire others to give."

"Happy Eid!"

On that day, Eva and Aya had the most fun and went on the best rides.

Ever since that special day, the two girls
became the best of friends.

I wonder, can Eid and Christmas coincide on the same day?

Muslims celebrate Eid twice a year. Eid Al-Fitr is celebrated after Ramadan, and Eid Al-Adha is celebrated on the last day of Hajj pilgrimage.

Since Christmas occurs on a fixed date every year, December 25, and Eid floats from year to year and occurs on different dates, then there is a possibility that one year Eid could fall on the same day as Christmas.

Christmas is based on the Solar calendar, whereas Eid is based on the Lunar calendar.

The Lunar calendar follows the moon's phases. In an evening, when the moon appears as a thin crescent, also called Hilal, it marks the end of a month and signals the start of a new month.

Made in United States
North Haven, CT
03 December 2021

11949535R00020